Nate the Great
and The
STICKY CASE

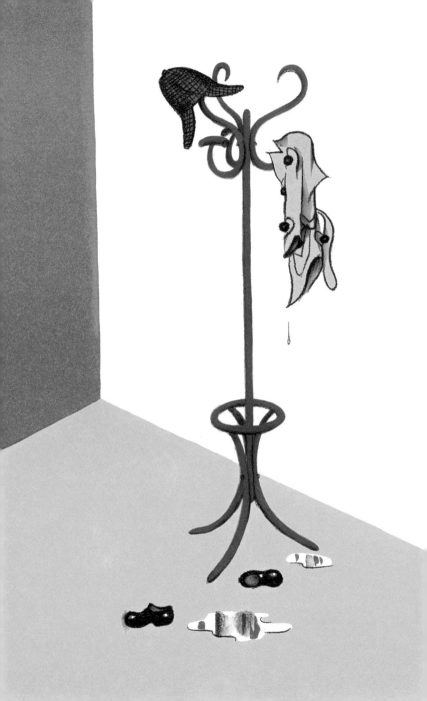

Nate the Great and The STICKY CASE

by Marjorie Weinman Sharmat

illustrations by Marc Simont

A Yearling Book

Visit us on the Web! www.randomhouse.com/kids

Educators and librarians, for a variety of teaching tools, visit us at
www.randomhouse.com/teachers

ISBN-13: 978-0-440-46289-7
ISBN-10: 0-440-46289-4

Reprinted by arrangement with the Putnam Publishing Group, Inc.
Printed in the United States of America
One Previous Edition
New Yearling Edition September 2006
65 64 63 62

To my sister Rosalind,
who let me name
Rosamond after her

I, Nate the Great,
was drying off
from the rain.
I was sitting
under a blanket
and reading a detective book.
My dog, Sludge, was sniffing it.

I was on page 33

when I heard a knock.

I opened the door.

Claude was there.

"I lost my best dinosaur,"

Claude said.

He was always losing things.

"This is your biggest loss yet,"

I said. "A dinosaur is huge.

How could you lose it?"

"My dinosaur is small,"

Claude said.

"It is a stegosaurus on a stamp.

Can you help me find it?"

"It is hard to find

something that small," I said.

"This will be a big case.

But I will take it.

Tell me, where was

the stegosaurus stamp

the last time you saw it?"

"It was on a table
in my house," Claude said.
"I was showing
all my dinosaur stamps
to my friends.
The stegosaurus stamp
was my favorite."
"Who are your friends?" I asked.
"Annie, Pip, Rosamond, and you.
But you weren't there,"
Claude added.

"Good thinking," I said.

"I, Nate the Great,

will go to your house

and look at your table."

I wrote a note to my mother.

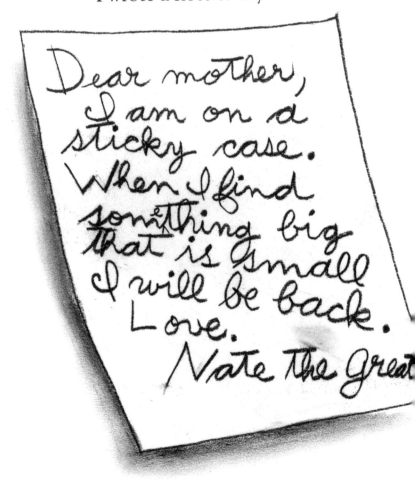

Dear mother,
I am on a
sticky case.
When I find
something big
that is small
I will be back.
Love.
Nate The Great

Claude and I went to his house.

He did not lose his way.

He showed me his table.

It had stamps all over it.

"Here are all of my stamps,"

Claude said. "Except for

the stegosaurus stamp."

I, Nate the Great,

saw a tyrannosaurus stamp.

I saw a brontosaurus stamp.

I saw an ichthyosaurus stamp.

I saw claws and jaws.

The stamps were ugly.

But that did not matter.

I had a case to solve.

I had a job to do.

"Where was the stegosaurus stamp
when it was on the table?"
I asked.
"Near the edge," Claude said.

"It must have fallen off,"
I said.
I looked on the floor
near the table.

The stegosaurus stamp
was not there.
I picked up a stamp
and showed it to Sludge.
"We must look for
a lost stamp," I said.
Sometimes Sludge is not
a great detective.
He tried to lick
the sticky side of the stamp.

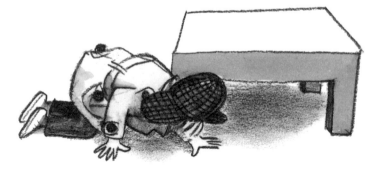

"*Look*. Don't lick," I said.
Sludge and I looked at, over,
under, and around everything
in Claude's house.
Then we looked again.
We did not find
the stegosaurus stamp.

I, Nate the Great,

turned to Claude.

"The stegosaurus stamp

is not in your house," I said.

"Tell me, when did you notice

the stamp was missing?"

"After everybody left," Claude said.

"Did everybody leave together?"

I asked.

"Yes," said Claude.

"Did everybody come together?"

I asked.

"No," said Claude.

"Annie and Rosamond came

to tell me that Rosamond

was going to have a yard sale.

Then it started to rain.

It rained for a long time.

So Annie and Rosamond stayed

and looked at my stamps.

When the rain stopped,
Pip came over.
He looked at my stamps too.
Then they all left together
to go to Rosamond's yard sale."
"Then I, Nate the Great,
must go to the yard sale too,"
I said.
"I must speak to everyone
who was in the room
with the stegosaurus stamp."
Sludge and I
went to Rosamond's house.
Rosamond was standing
in her yard
with her four cats under a sign:

"Are you selling your cats?" I asked.

"No," Rosamond said.

"I am selling and swapping

empty tuna fish cans,

slippers, spare cat hairs,

toothbrushes, pictures of milk,

spoons, and all sorts of things."

Sludge was sniffing.

"Do you have
a stegosaurus stamp?" I asked.

"No," Rosamond said.

"But I saw one at Claude's house,
near the edge of his table."

"Thank you," I said.

I started to leave.

"Please buy a cat hair
from my yard sale,"

Rosamond called. "They are only
a penny each."

I, Nate the Great, did not want
a cat hair.

But I gave Rosamond a penny.

"I will buy one cat hair,"
I said.

"I will give you
an extra one free,"

Rosamond said.

"Do you want hairs
from Big Hex, Little Hex,
Plain Hex, or Super Hex?"

"Surprise me," I said.

Rosamond took a hair from a box
that was marked "Big Hex"
and a hair from a box
that was marked "Super Hex."
She stuck the hairs
to a piece of tape.

"So you won't lose them,"
she said.

Sometimes Rosamond
has strange ideas.
This was one of them.

I saw Pip looking at
some empty tuna fish cans.
"Did you see a stegosaurus stamp
at the edge of Claude's table?"
I asked.
Pip doesn't say much.

He shook his head
up and down.

"Do you know where it is now?"
I asked.

Pip shook his head sideways.

"Thank you," I said.

I saw Annie and her dog, Fang.

"I am looking for Claude's
stegosaurus stamp," I said.

"What do you know about it?"

"I know that the stegosaurus
is pretty," Annie said.

"I know that it looks like Fang."

Annie turned toward Fang.

"Show us your stegosaurus smile,"
she said.

Fang opened his mouth.

I, Nate the Great,

knew it was time

to go home.

I said good-bye to Annie.

Sludge and I walked home slowly.

It was a good walk.

There were raindrops
on the tree leaves.

We saw ourselves in puddles.

We sniffed the clean air.

We saw a rainbow.

At home I made some pancakes.

I gave Sludge a bone.

We ate and thought.

Where was the stegosaurus stamp?

Nobody knew.

But the stamp was gone.

This was a sticky case.

I, Nate the Great, was stuck.

Then I thought,
Perhaps there is
something different
about a stegosaurus stamp.
Perhaps I should think
about the stegosaurus
instead of the stamp.
Suddenly I, Nate, felt great.
I had pancakes in my stomach
and a good idea in my head.

STEGOSAURUS
Giant Lizard

"Wait here, Sludge," I said.

"I have to go look

for information."

I went to the museum.

I saw a stegosaurus there.

I had to look up.

And up. And up.

The stegosaurus was big.

He was bigger than Fang.

His smile was uglier.

But he could not move.

He could not do anything.

I, Nate the Great,

was glad about that.

I learned about the stegosaurus.

He was a giant lizard.

He lived a long time ago.

He had two brains.

I, Nate the Great, wished

that I had two brains

and that one of them

would solve this case.

I walked home.

The signs of rain were gone

except for some puddles.

I thought hard.

What did I know

about the stegosaurus stamp?

I knew that Annie and Rosamond

went to Claude's house

and saw the stamp.

Then it rained for a long time.

I knew that
after the rain stopped,
Pip went to Claude's house
and saw the stamp too.
I knew the stamp had been
at the edge of Claude's table.
I knew it was not
in Claude's house now.

How did it get out

and where was it?

Seeing the big stegosaurus

had not helped the case.

Perhaps I had been thinking

wrong.

Perhaps I had forgotten

that there are two sides

to every stamp.

Perhaps I should think about

the sticky side

instead of the stegosaurus side.

"Think sticky," I said

when I walked inside

and saw Sludge.

Sludge was licking his dog bowl.

He had not been much help
on this case.
Or had he?
I remembered when
Sludge tried to lick
the sticky side of a stamp.
Sludge's wet tongue
would have made the stamp
very sticky.

A very sticky stamp . . . sticks!
Suddenly I knew that
Sludge was a great detective.
He knew that the sticky side
of the stamp
could be important.
I, Nate the Great, knew
that anything wet
would make a stamp
very sticky.
I thought of wet things.
I thought of drips and drops.
I thought of rain.
When Annie and Rosamond
went to Claude's house
it was not raining.

But when Pip went
to Claude's house
it had been raining
and stopped.
Raindrops were on the trees.
Puddles were on the sidewalk.
Hmm.
I, Nate the Great,
thought of puddles.
I thought of Pip
stepping in them.
I got a stamp from my desk
and put it on the floor.
I went outside
and stepped in a few puddles.
Then I went back inside

and stepped on the sticky side
of the stamp.
The stamp stuck to my shoe!
The same thing
must have happened
to the stegosaurus stamp
and Pip's shoe
at Claude's house.
Sludge had given me
the clue I needed.
Now I knew
that I had to see Pip's shoes.

We went to Pip's house.

I rang the bell.

Pip opened the door.

I looked down at his feet.

He was wearing slippers.

"Where are your shoes?" I asked.

Pip looked down at his feet.

He opened his mouth.

Then he said,

"My shoes were all wet

from the rain.

After I left Claude's house

I swapped them

for a pair of dry slippers

at Rosamond's yard sale.

I took the slippers

off the Swap Table

and put my shoes there."

"Thank you," I said.

Sludge and I went back

to Rosamond's yard sale.

We went up to the Swap Table.

"The sticky case

is almost over," I said.

But Pip's shoes were not there.

Rosamond came over.

"I hope you don't want to swap
your cat hairs," she said.

"I want Pip's shoes," I said.

"Where are they?"

"I just sold them to Annie
for ten cents," Rosamond said.

"It was my big sale of the day."

Sludge and I ran to Annie's house.

She was outside with Fang.

I saw two shoes.

One was on the ground.

The other was in Fang's mouth.

"Are these Pip's shoes?" I asked.

"They were," Annie said.

"I bought them
for Fang to chew."
I, Nate the Great,
saw the bottom of the shoe
Fang was chewing.
Something small, square, and dirty
was stuck to it.

At last I had found
the stegosaurus stamp.
But I, Nate the Great, knew
that finding was not everything.
Getting was important too.
I thought fast.
"Show me Fang's
stegosaurus smile," I said.
"Smile, Fang," Annie said.
Fang smiled.
The shoe fell to the ground.

I picked it up.

I, Nate the Great,

peeled off the stamp.

The case was solved.

We took the stegosaurus stamp

to Claude's house.

The stamp was dirty, sticky,

icky, and ugly.

But Claude was happy to get it.

Sludge and I walked home.
We were careful
not to step
in any puddles.

~Extra~ Fun Activities!

What's Inside

NATE'S NOTES: Dinosaurs

Did stegosaurus really have two brains? Scientists aren't sure about this. There are no dinosaur brains left for them to look at. Brains are soft. Unlike dinosaurs' bones, their brains didn't become fossils.

To learn about dino brains, scientists re-create them. Here's their "recipe": Coat the inside of a dino skull with plastic. Let dry. Pull the plastic out. Now you have a brain-shaped bag. Fill it with plaster. Let the plaster dry. Remove the bag to reveal the "brain."

Scientists say the stegosaurus wasn't smart. But it wasn't dumb, either! It was about as smart as an alligator.

What color were the dinos? That's another mystery! A good guess is that they were greenish brown, to blend in with their surroundings. Their skin may have looked like lizard skin.

Dino brains were too soft to become fossils—but dino poop wasn't!
Some scientists study poop fossils. They are called coprolites. They can tell us what dinos ate. Most dinos ate plants. A few ate other dinos.

Dinosaurs and people never lived at the same time. After the dinos died out, millions of years passed before the first humans appeared.

What was the earth like in dino time? Not completely different from the way it is today. Dinos saw pine trees growing. They munched on ferns. They shared lakes and rivers with crocodiles.

Some dinos laid eggs as big as footballs.

Dinos may have lived to be 300 years old!

Why did dinosaurs become extinct?
It may have happened after a giant
asteroid hit the earth. The rock
created huge windstorms, enormous
waves, and cloudy skies. Plants couldn't
survive the stormy weather. They died
out. The dinos didn't have enough to eat
so they died, too.

NATE'S NOTES: Stamps

The first U.S. stamps weren't sticky. People glued the stamps on letters. If they didn't have any glue, they used pins or sewed the stamps on.

The first sticky stamps were printed in 1847. A five-cent stamp showed Benjamin Franklin. Besides being an American statesman, Franklin was an inventor. He also help set up the post office. A ten-cent stamp showed George Washington, the first president of the United States.

The world's smallest post office is in Ochopee, Florida. The largest is in Chicago, Illinois.

Postal workers deliver about half a billion letters each day. They collect mail from 326,000 mailboxes. They deliver it to 250 million homes. The mail moves mostly on trucks, trains, and planes. But some homes are tough to reach. Letter carriers sometimes drop mail attached to parachutes. They ride snowmobiles to mountaintops. They pole boats and ride mules.

Anyone can propose an idea for a new stamp. Each year, thousands of people make suggestions. The post office picks about two dozen.

Some mail can't be delivered. The stamp falls off. There is no return address. What happens then? The letter goes to the dead letter office. A worker opens the letter. The worker looks for clues about who sent it. If the owner can't be found, the post office sells off any good stuff inside!

In 1958, the owner of the famous Hope Diamond gave it to a museum.
He mailed the diamond
from New York to Washington, D.C.
The stamps cost $2.44.
The diamond
was worth $1 million.

A Boston tavern was the country's first post office. By 1788, there were seventy-five post offices.

Horse-drawn carriages carried the mail.

So did riders on horseback. By 1860, there were 28,000 post offices. You could mail a letter in New York. It would get to California four weeks later.

Ten Fun Things to Look at with a Magnifying Glass

Nate uses a magnifying glass to find clues. Claude uses one to look at his stamps. You probably have a magnifying glass at home. Find it. Or buy one at the drugstore. Then start looking! Here are ten cool things to examine:

1. A postage stamp. What do you notice about the colors on the stamp? Are they solid? No, they're made up of many tiny dots.

2. A flight feather. Flight feathers come from birds' wings. Each feather has a shaft running up the middle. On each side of the shaft are hundreds of barbs. Can you see the tiny hooks on each barb? Thanks to these hooks, birds can "zip" the barbs together. That helps them fly. They "unzip" the barbs to clean their feathers.

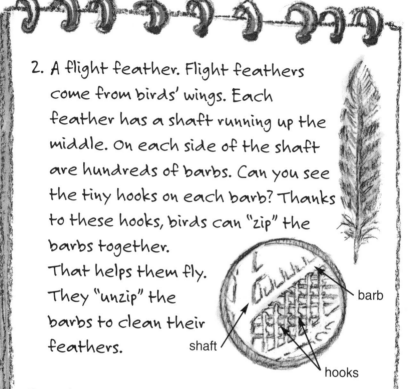

barb

shaft

hooks

3. Salt. Are grains of salt all the same shape? No, they're all different.

4. A leaf. Has anything been nibbling on this leaf? Can you see any insect eggs?

5. Your fingertip. Check out the fancy whorls (patterns of thin, curving grooves). Everyone's fingertips have different patterns! Detectives like fingerprints. They help figure out who was where when.

6. A compact disc or DVD. Shine a bright light on your CD or DVD. How many colors can you see? The colors may remind you of a soap bubble.

7. A dead bug. Look for a dead fly or bee on a windowsill. Is its body covered with a hard shell or with fuzz? Can you find a clue to the way the bug died?

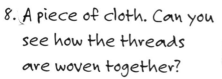

8. A piece of cloth. Can you see how the threads are woven together?

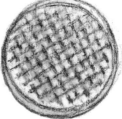

9. A live ant. You can find ants in your backyard or in a nearby park. A crack in the sidewalk is a good place to hunt. What color is the ant you found? How many body parts does it have?

10. Something else YOU find!

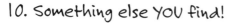

A Map of a Stamp

Here are the parts of a stamp:

The country's name: More than 260 countries around the world print stamps. Almost every country prints its name on the stamp. Great Britain is the only country that doesn't. Why is it different? Great Britain was the first country to print stamps. It puts a picture of the queen's face on each one.

The face value: This is how much you pay for the stamp at the post office. An old stamp can be much more—or much less—valuable than a new one.

The design: Some stamps honor famous people. Others celebrate important events.

The holes: Tiny holes make it easier to tear apart a sheet or roll of stamps.

The cancellation: This shows that the stamp has been used and stops anyone from using it again. The cancellation may consist of wavy lines, straight lines, or other marks.

Four Serious Stamps

Stamp collectors search for unusual stamps. They never stick their stamps on envelopes. Some rare stamps are worth a lot of money. Read on to learn about a few of the world's most valuable stamps.

Stamp #1: Sweden Three-Skilling Banco
(Yellow Color Error)
When printed: 1855
Number surviving: 1
Last sold: 1996
The price: $2.3 million

A skilling is a Swedish coin. Back in 1855, stamps that cost three skillings were printed on green paper. Someone messed up. They printed some on yellow paper. Only one of the yellow stamps survives.

Stamp #2: Post Office Mauritius
When printed: 1847
Number surviving: about 30
Last sold: 1993
The price: $3.8 million (for two)

This is another story about a printer messing up. This time, it happened on Mauritius. That's an island in the Indian Ocean. The printer wrote "Post Office" on some stamps. They were supposed to say "Post Paid." People bought more than two hundred of the stamps. Someone stuck two on an envelope. In 1993, that envelope sold for $3.8 million.

Stamp #3: Hawaiian Missionaries Two-cent
When printed: 1851
Number surviving: 16
Last sold: 1995
The price: $1.9 million for an envelope with
one two-cent stamp

Hawaii's first stamps came out in 1851.
They were mostly used by missionaries,
people who travel to teach other people
about their religion. The printer used thin
paper. Few of these stamps survived.

Stamp #4: British Guiana One-cent
(Black on Magenta)
When printed: 1856
Number surviving: 1
Last sold: 1980
The price: $935,000

The South American republic of
Guyana was once a colony called
British Guiana. Back in 1856, the colony
ran out of stamps. Nobody wanted to
wait for new stamps from England. So a
local printer made some. He used
magenta (reddish) paper with black ink.
The stamps showed a sailboat. The
corners of the stamps were snipped off.
Only one has survived. That's why it's so
valuable.

Dinosaur Egg Recipe

Make these eggs. Get together with some friends who love dinosaurs. Give out the eggs. Have a good time. (Just don't eat the eggs!)

GET TOGETHER:

- a mixing bowl
- $2\frac{1}{2}$ cups flour
- $2\frac{1}{2}$ cups used coffee grounds
- $1\frac{1}{2}$ cups salt
- 1 cup sand
- water
- small plastic dinosaurs*

*You can find these at toy stores.

MAKE YOUR DINO EGGS:

1. In the bowl, mix together the flour, coffee grounds, salt, and sand.
2. Slowly add water. Stir. Keep adding water until the mixture holds together.
3. Cover a plastic dinosaur with the mixture. Form the mixture into an egg shape.

4. Let dry at least 24 hours. Longer is better.
5. You may need to help your dinosaur "hatch" with a rock or a hammer.

How to Make Yard-Sale Dinosaur Lollipops

Rosamond sells cat hairs at her yard sale. Next time you have a yard sale, sell these dinosaur pops. They'll be much more popular.

Get an adult to help you with this recipe.

GET TOGETHER:

- dinosaur lollipop molds*
- cooking spray
- enough chocolate to fill your molds (usually two chocolate bars is enough to make four lollipops)
- a microwave oven and a bowl, or a stovetop and a double boiler
- oven mitts
- lollipop sticks*
- sandwich bags
- curling ribbon
- scissors

You can find these at craft stores. Or buy them online.

MAKE YOUR DINO POPS:

1. Spray the molds with cooking spray. Set aside.
2. Break the chocolate into small pieces.

3. IF USING A STOVETOP:
   Fill the bottom part of a double boiler halfway with water. Place the chocolate pieces in the top part. Warm over medium heat until the chocolate melts.

   IF USING A MICROWAVE:
   Place the chocolate pieces in the bowl. Heat at half power for one minute. Stir. The chocolate will still be lumpy. Heat for another minute. Stir. Continue heating and stirring until all the lumps melt.

4. Carefully pour the chocolate into the molds. Use the oven mitts! The chocolate will be hot.
5. Put the sticks into the molds.
6. Chill the molds in the refrigerator for three hours.

7. Remove the dinosaurs
   from the molds by tugging
   gently on the sticks.

8. Put each lollipop in a sandwich bag.
   Tie the bag closed with a piece of ribbon.
   Curl the ribbon
   with scissors.

Have you helped solve all Nate the Great's mysteries?

❑ **Nate the Great**: Meet Nate, the great detective, and join him as he uses incredible sleuthing skills to solve his first big case.

❑ **Nate the Great Goes Undercover**: Who— or what—is raiding Oliver's trash every night? Nate bravely hides out in his friend's garbage can to catch the smelly crook.

❑ **Nate the Great and the Lost List**: Nate loves pancakes, but who ever heard of cats eating them? Is a strange recipe at the heart of this mystery?

❑ **Nate the Great and the Phony Clue**: Against ferocious cats, hostile adversaries, and a sly phony clue, Nate struggles to prove that he's still the world's greatest detective.

❑ **Nate the Great and the Sticky Case**: Nate is stuck with his stickiest case yet as he hunts for his friend Claude's valuable stegosaurus stamp.

❑ **Nate the Great and the Missing Key**: Nate isn't afraid to look anywhere—even under the nose of his friend's ferocious dog, Fang—to solve the case of the missing key.

❑ **Nate the Great and the Stolen Base**: It's not easy to track down a stolen base, and Nate's hunt leads him to some strange places before he finds himself at bat once more.

❑ **Nate the Great and the Pillowcase**: When a pillowcase goes missing, Nate must venture into the dead of night to search for clues. Everyone sleeps easier knowing Nate the Great is on the case!

❑ **Nate the Great and the Mushy Valentine**: Nate hates mushy stuff. But when someone leaves a big heart taped to Sludge's doghouse, Nate must help his favorite pooch discover his secret admirer.

❑ **Nate the Great and the Tardy Tortoise**: Where did the mysterious green tortoise in Nate's yard come from? Nate needs all his patience to follow this slow . . . slow . . . clue.

❑ **Nate the Great and the Crunchy Christmas**: It's Christmas, and Fang, Annie's scary dog, is not feeling jolly. Can Nate find Fang's crunchy Christmas mail before Fang crunches on *him*?

❑ **Nate the Great Saves the King of Sweden**: Can Nate solve his *first-ever* international case without leaving his own neighborhood?

❑ **Nate the Great and Me: The Case of the Fleeing Fang**: A surprise Happy Detective Day party is great fun for Nate until his friend's dog disappears! Help Nate track down the missing pooch, and learn all the tricks of the trade in a special fun section for aspiring detectives.

❑ **Nate the Great and the Monster Mess**: Nate loves his mother's deliciously spooky Monster Cookies, but the recipe has vanished! This is one case Nate and his growling stomach can't afford to lose.

❑ **Nate the Great, San Francisco Detective**: Nate visits his cousin Olivia Sharp in the big city, but it's no vacation. Can he find a lost joke book in time to save the world?

❑ **Nate the Great and the Big Sniff**: Nate depends on his dog, Sludge, to help him solve all his cases. But Nate is on his own this time, because Sludge has disappeared! Can Nate solve the case and recover his canine buddy?

❑ **Nate the Great on the Owl Express**: Nate boards a train to guard Hoot, his cousin Olivia Sharp's pet owl. Then Hoot vanishes! Can Nate find out *whooo* took the feathered creature?